IF I
WERE
IN CHARGE
OF THE
WRLD

and other worries

BOOKS BY JUDITH VIORST

IF I WERE IN CHARGE OF THE WORLD

and other worries

poems for children and their parents by

JUDITH VIORST

ILLUSTRATED BY LYNNE CHERRY

Aladdin Books
Macmillan Publishing Company
New York

Some of the poems appearing in this volume were originally
published in Redbook magazine.

DESIGNED BY DOROTHY FALL

Aladdin Books
Macmillan Publishing Company
866 Third Avenue, New York, NY 10022
Collier Macmillan Canada, Inc.

First Aladdin Books edition

Printed in the United States of America

A hardcover edition of IF I WERE IN CHARGE OF THE WORLD
and other worries is available from Atheneum.

10   9   8

Library of Congress Cataloging-in-Publication Data

Viorst, Judith
   If I were in charge of the world and other worries.

   Summary: Forty-one poems reveal a variety of secret
thoughts, worries, and wishes.
   1. Children's poetry, American. [1. American poetry]
I. Cherry, Lynne, ill. II. Title.
PS3572.I6I36   1987   811'.54   87-14463
ISBN 0-689-70770-3 (pbk.)

For
Hanna and Peter Altman
and
Sally and Bob Pitofsky

CONTENTS

CONSULTANTS

Alexander Viorst, Chief Consultant
Nicholas Viorst
Anthony Viorst
Amy Oberdorfer
Lisa Schorr
Elizabeth Pitofsky

WISHES AND WORRIES

IF I WERE IN CHARGE OF THE WORLD

If I were in charge of the world
I'd cancel oatmeal,
Monday mornings,
Allergy shots, and also
Sara Steinberg.

If I were in charge of the world
There'd be brighter night lights,
Healthier hamsters, and
Basketball baskets forty-eight inches lower.

If I were in charge of the world
You wouldn't have lonely.
You wouldn't have clean.
You wouldn't have bedtimes.
Or "Don't punch your sister."
You wouldn't even have sisters.

If I were in charge of the world
A chocolate sundae with whipped cream and nuts
        would be a vegetable.
All 007 movies would be G.
And a person who sometimes forgot to brush,
And sometimes forgot to flush,
Would still be allowed to be
In charge of the world.

3

BERTHA'S WISH

I wish that I didn't have freckles on my face.
I wish that my stomach went in instead of out.
I wish that he would stand on top of the tallest
     building and shout,
"I love you, Amanda."

One more wish: I wish my name was Amanda.

I WOULDN'T BE AFRAID

I wouldn't be afraid to fight a demon or a dragon,
    if you'd dare me.
I wouldn't be afraid of witches, warlocks, trolls, or giants.
Just worms scare me.

FIFTEEN, MAYBE SIXTEEN, THINGS TO WORRY ABOUT

My pants could maybe fall down when I dive off the diving board.
My nose could maybe keep growing and never quit.
Miss Brearly could ask me to spell words like *stomach* and *special*.
    (*Stumick* and *speshul?*)
I could play tag all day and always be "it."

Jay Spievack, who's fourteen feet tall, could want to fight me.
My mom and my dad—like Ted's—could want a divorce.
Miss Brearly could ask me a question about Afghanistan.
    (Who's Afghanistan?)
Somebody maybe could make me ride a horse.

My mother could maybe decide that I needed more liver.
My dad could decide that I needed less TV.
Miss Brearly could say that I have to write script and stop printing.

Chris could decide to stop being friends with me.

The world could maybe come to an end on next Tuesday.
The ceiling could maybe come crashing on my head.
I maybe could run out of things for me to worry about.
And then I'd have to do my homework instead.

SOME THINGS DON'T
MAKE ANY SENSE AT ALL

My mom says I'm her sugarplum.
My mom says I'm her lamb.
My mom says I'm completely perfect
Just the way I am.
My mom says I'm a super-special wonderful terrific
     little guy.
My mom just had another baby.
Why?

CATS AND OTHER PEOPLE

MY CAT

My cat isn't stuck up,
Even though
He's the handsomest cat in
    the world,
And smart,
And brave,
And climbs the highest trees.
My cat will sit on your lap and
    let you pet him.
He won't mind.
He thinks human beings are
Almost as good
As he is.

STANLEY THE FIERCE

Stanley the Fierce
Has a chipped front tooth
And clumps of spiky hair.
And his hands are curled into
    two fat fists
And his arms are bulgy and bare.
And his smile is a tight little
    mean little smile
And his eyes give a shivery glare.
And I hear that he goes for seventeen days
Without changing his underwear.

But I don't think I'll ask him.

HARVEY

Harvey doesn't laugh about how I stay short while everybody grows.
Harvey remembers I like jellybeans—except black.
Harvey lends me shirts I don't have to give back.
I'm scared of ghosts and only Harvey knows.

Harvey thinks I will when I say someday I will marry Margie Rose.
Harvey shares his lemonade—sip for sip.
He whispers "zip" when I forget to zip.
He swears I don't have funny-looking toes.

Harvey calls me up when I'm in bed with a sore throat and runny nose.
Harvey says I'm nice—but not *too* nice.
And if there is a train to Paradise,
I won't get on it unless Harvey goes.

THE LIZZIE PITOFSKY POEM

I can't get enoughsky
Of Lizzie Pitofsky.
I love her so much that it hurts.
I want her so terrible
I'd give her my gerbil
Plus twenty-two weeks of desserts.

I know that it's lovesky
'Cause Lizzie Pitofsky
Is turning me into a saint.
I smell like a rose,
I've stopped picking my nose,
And I practically never say ain't.

I don't push and shovesky
'Cause Lizzie Pitofsky
Likes boys who are gentle and kind.
I'm not throwing rocks
And I'm changing my socks
(And to tell you the truth I don't mind).

Put tacks in my shoes,
Feed me vinegar juice,
And do other mean bad awful stuffsky.
But promise me this:
I won't die without kiss-
Ing my glorious Lizzie Pitofsky.

WHO'S WHO

Paula is the prettiest—the whole sixth grade agrees.
Jean's the genius—that is undeniable.
Most popular is Amy. Most admired is Louise.
But as for me, they say I'm most . . . reliable.

Lisa's the best listener—she always lends an ear.
And all the boys say Meg's the most desirable.
Gwen's the giggliest—but everybody thinks that's dear.
Who thinks it's dear to be the most reliable?

Jody and Rebecca tie for cleverest. Marie
Is best at sports (and also most perspirable).
Cathy is the richest—she's been saving since she's three.
But who'll save me from being most reliable?

I'd rather be most mischievous. I'd rather be most deep.
I'd rather—and I'll swear this on a Bible—
Be known as most peculiar. Nothing puts the world to sleep
Like someone who is known as most reliable.

NIGHTS

NIGHT SCARE

There aren't any ghosts.
There aren't any.
There aren't any gho—
Well . . . not too many.

NIGHTMARE

Beautiful beautiful Beverly
Has asked me to a dance.
And I am dressed
In all my best:
My purple shirt,
My buckskin vest,
My cowboy boots,
My—oops!
Where are my pants?

NIGHT FUN

I hear eating.
I hear drinking.
I hear music.
I hear laughter.
Fun is something
Grownups never have
Before my bedtime.
Only after.

THOUGHTS ON GETTING OUT OF A NICE WARM BED IN AN ICE-COLD HOUSE TO GO TO THE BATHROOM AT THREE O'CLOCK IN THE MORNING

Maybe life was better
When I used to be a wetter.

SPRING FEVER

JUST BEFORE SPRINGTIME

The birds are still out of town,
The branches still bare.
The earth is still colored brown.
I don't care!
I don't care!
I can smell the green smell in the air—it comes
Just before springtime.

The wind still bends my head low.
Slush sloshes my boots.
Everyone's talking more snow.
I hear flutes!
I hear flutes!
It's the music that says, World wake up—it comes
Just before springtime.

The ground hog's shadow was long.
Bad winter in store.
That ground hog legend is wrong.
I know more!
I know more!
There's a sweetness that licks at my mouth,
And it tastes not of North, but of South.
There's a vision that fills up my eyes
With wings making waves in warm skies.
There's a softness that writes on my skin
The announcement that spring's coming in.
Earth-bird-tree
I am you.
You are me.
We are one!
We are one!
In that gentle moment that comes
Just before springtime.

WEIRD!

My sister Stephanie's in love.
(I thought she hated boys.)
My brother had a yard sale and
Got rid of all his toys.
My mother started jogging, and
My dad shaved off his beard.
It's spring—and everyone but me
Is acting really weird.

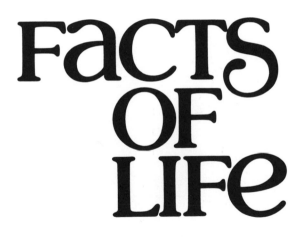

SHORT LOVE POEM

It's hard to love
The tallest girl
When you're the shortest guy,
For every time
You try to look
Your true love in the eye
You see
Her bellybutton.

LEARNING

I'm learning to say thank you.
And I'm learning to say please.
And I'm learning to use Kleenex,
Not my sweater, when I sneeze.
And I'm learning not to dribble.
And I'm learning not to slurp.
And I'm learning (though it sometimes
        really hurts me)
Not to burp.
And I'm learning to chew softer
When I eat corn on the cob.
And I'm learning that it's much
Much easier to be a slob.

I'M NOT

I'm not the biggest or smallest or shortest or tallest
    or fastest or slowest or meanest or sweetest, and
I'm not the oldest or youngest or smartest or dumbest,
    but most of all

I'M

NoT

the

Neatest.

MENDING

A giant hand inside my chest
Stretches out and takes
My heart within its mighty grasp
And squeezes till it breaks.

A gentle hand inside my chest,
With mending tape and glue,
Patches up my heart until
It's almost good as new.

I ought to know by now that
Broken hearts will heal again.
But while I wait for glue and tape,
The pain!
The pain!
The pain!

... AND THE PRINCESS WAS ASTONISHED TO SEE THE UGLY FROG TURN INTO A HANDSOME PRINCE

He worshiped me.
And he waited on me.
And he fetched my golden ball.
And he told me I was definitely
The loveliest princess of all.
And when he ate from my golden plate
He practically fainted with joy.
Oh, he was a very pleasant frog.
He's a very conceited boy.

...AND THEN THE PRINCE KNELT DOWN AND TRIED TO PUT THE GLASS SLIPPER ON CINDERELLA'S FOOT

I really didn't notice that he had a funny nose.
And he certainly looked better all dressed up in fancy clothes.
He's not nearly as attractive as he seemed the other night.
So I think I'll just pretend that this glass slipper feels too tight.

. . . AND ALTHOUGH THE LITTLE MERMAID
SACRIFICED EVERYTHING TO WIN THE LOVE OF THE PRINCE,
THE PRINCE (ALAS) DECIDED TO WED ANOTHER

I left the castle of my mer-king father,
Where seaweed gardens sway in pearly sand.
I left behind sweet sisters and kind waters
To seek a prince's love upon the land.

My tongue was payment for the witch's potion
(And never would I sing sea songs again).
My tail became two human legs to dance on,
But I would always dance with blood and pain.

I risked more than my life to make him love me.
The prince preferred another for his bride.
I always hate the ending to this story:
They lived together happily; I died.

But I have some advice for modern mermaids
Who wish to save great sorrow and travail:
Don't give up who you are for love of princes.
He might have liked me better with my tail.

...AND AFTER MANY YEARS, A BRAVE PRINCE CAME AT LAST TO RESCUE THE PRINCESS

Down in the courtyard
Beneath my high window,
Victor of wizards and hazards and mazes,
Beautiful, proud on your horse,
You are calling my name.

Often I dreamed
As I sat by my window,
Dreamed of the prince and the horse and the journey.
Gray day in gray day dissolved,
But my prince never came.

Often I dreamed.
But the brambles grew thicker
Until I became an old princess, accustomed
To daydreams, the safety of towers,
This room, and this chair.

And now you are calling
Beneath my high window,
Victor of wizards and hazards and mazes,
Beautiful, proud—
How you shine in these shadows!

No, my prince.
No, my dear.
I will not let down my hair.

WORDS

SECRETS

Anne told Beth.
And Beth told me.
And I am telling you.
But don't tell Sue—
You know she can't
Keep secrets.

TALKING

They tell me that I talk too much.
I'm trying not to talk too much.
But, oh, it's hard to take time out
When there's so much to talk about:
How long it took to pull my tooth.
How hard it is to tell the truth.
Why steel is not as nice as trees.
Why Brian has such scabby knees.
Twelve sights I saw in Williamsburg.
The definition of an *erg*.
Why roller skates are not my style.
Six reasons goldfish never smile.
How come I'd rather freeze than roast.
And ten things that I love the most:
The mustache on my father's face.
Fires in the fireplace.
Any book by Judy Blume.
Never cleaning up my room.
Every single valentine
Sent to me by Chris Romine.
Drummers in a marching band.
Ferry rides,
The Redskins,
Poems, and
Talking.

SOMETIMES POEMS

Sometimes poems are
Short and fat
    And have a
    Double chin.

The
Poems
I
Write
Don't
Look
Like
That.
My
Poems
Are
Tall
And
Thin.
Except
The
Day
I
Sat,
Then
Looked;
Instead
Of
Looked,
Then
Sat:

And squashed one flat.

APOLOGY

It's hard to say "I'm sorry,"
Although I'm feeling sorry.
The "s" always sticks in my throat.
And "I made a big mistake"
Would produce a bellyache
That might last till I was old enough to vote.

"Please forgive me" sounds real good.
And I'd say it if I could,
But between the "forgive" and the "please"
I would have to go to bed
With a pounding in my head
And a very shaky feeling in my knees.

"I was wrong" seems oh so right.
But it gives me such a fright
That my "was" always turns into "ain't."
So I hope you'll take this rhyme
As my way of saying "I'm
Really sorry." Now excuse me while I faint.

Thanks and no Thanks

NO

No. I refuse to.
No. I don't choose to.
No. I most certainly don't.
You've made a mistake
If you thought you could make
Me. No no no—I won't.

No. You could beat me.
No. You could eat me
Up from my head to my toes,
And inside your belly,
Loudly and yelly,
I'd keep saying no's.

No. You could sock me,
Feed me some broccoli,
Tickle me till I turned blue,
But in between giggles
And sniggles and wriggles
I'd say no to you.

No. You could tease me,
Please, pretty please, me,
Cry till your eyes washed away.
You could beg till you're old,
But I'd look at you cold.
En-oh is what I'd say.

No. You could shove me.
No. You could love me
With kisses all squishy and wet.
You could scratch me with claws
But I'd say no, because
. . . because . . . because . . .
I forget!

THANK-YOU NOTE

I wanted small pierced earrings (gold).
You gave me slippers (gray).
My mother said that she would scold
Unless I wrote to say
How much I liked them.

Not much.

WHAT PRICE GLORY?

I stood on a stage
And they gave me a medal
For being the
Best of the Bunch.
Then Ricky Gesumaria came by
And ate it up for lunch,
With mustard, a pickle, two slices of rye,
And a very nasty crr-rr-unch.

I stood on a stage
And they gave me a trophy
For being the
Top of the Heap.
I waited for cheers but the audience
Had fallen fast asleep,
Except for Joshua, who yelled,
"No trophies for that creep!"

I stood on a stage
And they gave me a plaque that
Said I was the
Star of the show.
It weighed a hundred pounds. Max Goldfarb
Dropped it on my toe.
And the next time someone calls my name
And wants me to stand on the stage
And get some prizes . . .
I'll still go.

MOTHER DOESN'T WANT A DOG

Mother doesn't want a dog.
Mother says they smell,
And never sit when you say sit,
Or even when you yell.
And when you come home late at night
And there is ice and snow,
You have to go back out because
The dumb dog has to go.

Mother doesn't want a dog.
Mother says they shed,
And always let the strangers in
And bark at friends instead,
And do disgraceful things on rugs,
And track mud on the floor,
And flop upon your bed at night
And snore their doggy snore.

Mother doesn't want a dog.
She's making a mistake.
Because, more than a dog, I think
She will not want this snake.

WICKED THOUGHTS

WICKED THOUGHTS

The meanest girl I've ever met
Is Mary Ellen Wright,
And if a lion came along and
Ate her with one bite,
I'd cry and cry and cry and cry.
(But just to be polite).

MORE WICKED THOUGHTS

Jennifer Jill has the brainiest of all the brains
    in class.
Jennifer Jill has the prettiest of the faces.
Jennifer Jill has a real gold watch and ten best friends
    and the leading role in the Christmas play.
(I'm glad that Jennifer Jill has to wear braces.)

AND SOME MORE WICKED THOUGHTS

In every race I've ever run
I'm number two; Joe's number one.
There's awful things that I could do
To make me one and make Joe two.
(But I won't even think of them).

SUMMER'S END

One by one the petals drop.
There's nothing that can make them stop.
You cannot beg a rose to stay.
Why does it have to be that way?

The butterflies I used to chase
Have gone off to some other place.
I don't know where. I only know
I wish they didn't have to go.

And all the shiny afternoons
So full of birds and big balloons
And ice cream melting in the sun
Are done. I do not want them done.

GOOD-BYE, SIX—HELLO, SEVEN

I'm getting a higher bunk bed.
And I'm getting a bigger bike.
And I'm getting to cross Connecticut Avenue
    all by myself, if I like.
And I'm getting to help do dishes.
And I'm getting to weed the yard.
And I'm getting to think that seven
    could be hard.

TEDDY BEAR POEM

I threw away my teddy bear,
The one that lost his eye.
I threw him in the garbage pail
(I thought I heard him cry.)

I've had that little teddy bear
Since I was only two.
But I'm much bigger now and
I've got better things to do

Than play with silly teddy bears.
And so I said good-bye
And threw him in the garbage pail.
(Who's crying—he, or I?)

REMEMBER ME ?

What will they say
When I've gone away:
He was handsome? He was fun?
He shared his gum? He wasn't
Too dumb or too smart? He
Played a good game of volley ball?
Or will they only say
He stepped in the dog doo
At Jimmy Altman's party?

SINCE HANNA MOVED AWAY

The tires on my bike are flat.
The sky is grouchy gray.
At least it sure feels like that
Since Hanna moved away.

Chocolate ice cream tastes like prunes.
December's come to stay.
They've taken back the Mays and Junes
Since Hanna moved away.

Flowers smell like halibut.
Velvet feels like hay.
Every handsome dog's a mutt
Since Hanna moved away.

Nothing's fun to laugh about.
Nothing's fun to play.
They call me, but I won't come out
Since Hanna moved away.

MY—OH WOW!—BOOK

I'm lying here
and I'm sick in bed
with a terrible
horrible
pain in my head,
and these funny bumps
that my ma says look
like the chicken pox,
and my—oh wow!—book,
and some Band-Aids (six)
for the spots I hurt
where I fell on stones
when I missed the dirt,
and my—oh wow!—book,
and my swollen thumb
that the door slammed on,
and this aching stom-
ach from fifths on root beer
and thirds on pie,
and my—oh wow!—book,
which I'm not gonna die
till I finish.

INDEX